The Mermaid's adventure

Daisy and Azalea

By Diana Molly

Introduction

When Daisy and Azalea find a bottle with strange notes under the ocean, they don't have any idea that the biggest adventure of their life is about to begin. While they seek the advice of their teachers, face the strange nature of Beyondness and try to walk, the curious and beautiful mermaids understand the value of kindness and bravery, when they're faced with a dilemma. Will they choose to rescue the prince, or will the fear win after all?

Make decisions, think with and worry about the mermaid sisters in the breathtaking pages of this adventurous book full of action and humor

Chapter 1

The Bottle

"Azalea?" Daisy called her elder sister, brushing her long blond hair in front of the mirror in their bedroom. The ten-year-old pretty mermaid smiled at the reflection of her blue sparkling mermaid tail and her purple top, and then turned to look at her sister who was reading a book, lying in the cushioned pearl shell, her turquoise tail curled up under her, and her long brown hair spread all around the shell.

Azalea was so much engrossed in her reading that she didn't even lookup.

"Let's go to play, please," Daisy said, coming to her sister. "You will read the book later."

"Oh, Daisy," Azalea said, her eyes still on the book, "I still have a few chapters to go before I finish the book. It's such an interesting book!"

"Really? What's it about?" Daisy came forward.

"It's about Beyondness," Azalea said. "About the life there. I can't stop reading. Every time I read, I discover new things."

"Yes, I love books about Beyondness, too," Daisy said, smiling. "They're my most favorite books. But you can continue reading after we return. The weather is so great in Clover today. Please, let's go outside and play a little."

Putting the book aside, Azalea got up from the shell, stretched lazily and swam towards the door.

"Let's go, then," she said joyfully.

The two mermaid sisters swam out of their pretty house that was like a flower. All the houses were like flowers in their town Clover under the ocean.

Daisy and Azalea liked to play outside, especially during the summer vacations, when there was no school and no lessons.

A pretty pink fish came swimming by before they could think of a game.

"Wow! Did you see that?" Daisy asked her sister. "I haven't seen such a pretty fish in my life!" Daisy started to follow the fish.

"Where are you going, Daisy? Come back!" Azalea calls.

"Let's follow this fish, Azalea," Daisy called. She was already far from Azalea. Shrugging, she followed Daisy.

"Listen, Daisy; we shouldn't go far from our house – mom and dad will worry!" Azalea said.

"They won't worry because we're not getting lost. So what that you're two years older than me?" Daisy said stubbornly. "You must not boss me around."

"Okay, but mom and dad will worry!"

"We won't be late for dinner," Daisy said, smiling. Azalea also smiled. The two sisters held hands and swam after the pink fish. Soon they were out of Clover and were swimming towards an unfamiliar place, which was darker than their town and deserted, too. They stopped and looked around: the pink fish swam happily away, but they didn't follow the fish anymore. They were looking around, their eyes wide in surprise and awe.

"Look, Azalea, we have never been out of Clover before," Daisy said, her eyes sparkling. "Let's explore this place."

"Um… are you sure, Daisy?" Azalea said, frowning. "I don't think it's a good idea."

"This is not scary at all, Azalea! This is an adventure!" Daisy said, giggling and tagging on her arm. Hesitating, Azalea swam with Daisy to explore the surroundings.

"All right, Daisy, but we'll not stay here long. It's dark and deserted here, and it's out of town," Azalea said, but Daisy suddenly gasped.

"Hey, Azalea, what's that?" Daisy swam fast to a glass bottle.

"Don't touch it!" Azalea screamed; her eyes wide.

"Why?" Daisy asked, taking the bottle and looking at it intently. There was something inside it. "I wonder what this is," she said, opening the bottle and putting inside her two fingers, trying to take it out. It was a piece of old cloth.

"Azalea, look here!" Daisy exclaimed, brandishing the cloth in her hands. "I've found this inside the bottle!"

Azalea swam hastily to her sister and looked at the cloth. It was a small piece of cloth, and there was something written on it.

"Give it to me," Azalea said, taking the cloth from Daisy's hands and examining it closely. "Something's written here."

Daisy and Azalea tried to read what was written on the cloth in dark ink.

"'I am Prince Zeke from Penetoland. I was flying in my air balloon when it got damaged and I descended onto a strange island. Now I'm trapped here and can't come out. Please whoever finds this letter, come and rescue me, as the Kingdom of Penetoland will stay without their Prince.'" Azalea read aloud.

Daisy's eyes were shining. "Wow, Azalea! Can you imagine that?"

Azalea was looking at her sister with wide-open eyes, unable to say anything. Daisy took the cloth from her hands and turned it over. There was a map drawn there in the same dark ink.

"Azalea!" she shrieked. "Look here! This looks like a map!"

"What!" Azalea exclaimed.

The sisters were silently looking at each other for a while. Daisy's eyes were shining with happiness, while Azalea looked worried and thoughtful.

"Daisy, I think the Prince is from Beyondness," Azalea said.

"Beyondness?!" Daisy shrieked. "I think you're right, Azalea! Penetoland is in Beyondness. I've read about it somewhere in my books."

"Daisy, we must make sure that the Prince is rescued," she said.

"Of course we must!" Daisy yelled. "Can you imagine, Azalea?! A prince! I wonder if he's good-looking."

"No, no, wait, Daisy," Azalea said. "At first we must go and tell our parents about this. What if it's dangerous?"

"Are you crazy, Azalea?" Daisy's eyes became round. "If we tell them, then they won't let us rescue the prince."

"Well, I guess you're right. But how can we go and rescue the prince?"

"I don't know," Daisy said, scratching her head. "The map is probably for the island. We can take the map and swim to the island. Oh, Azalea! It's so exciting! It's a real adventure!"

"Yes, sounds like it," Azalea said, still looking thoughtful. "But there are still questions in my head."

"Like what?" Daisy said impatiently.

"Like, how are we going to find the island," Azalea said, counting on her fingers. "How are we going to move on the island, if all we have are tails? I've read in my books about Beyondness that humans don't have tails at all. They have a pair of things called legs."

"We'll think something, don't worry," Daisy said. "But no matter what, we must not tell anyone about it, because they will go and rescue the prince themselves, and they won't let us do it alone."

"I also think so…" Azalea said. Then her face brightened. "I think I know what to do!"

Chapter 2
Myth or Reality?

Daisy came closer to her sister, to hear well.

"Even though there's no school now in Clover, our Teacher of Worldology is still there, isn't he?" Azalea said, smiling. "Teacher Arlo can help us."

"Please don't tell me you're going to tell him to help us!" Daisy's smile faded.

"No, no, of course, I'm not!" Azalea said. "I'm only going to ask him what the map means."

"Hmm, sounds like a great plan!"

"See? Being two years older than you has its advantages," Azalea said, as they swam back to Clover, taking the piece of cloth with them.

The sisters were excited. Even though Azalea was a bit careful, she was also looking forward to the grand adventure they were going to have soon. They reached Clover and swam straight to the school, which was a pretty building like a flower. As they were expecting, Teacher Arlo was there, sitting magnificently in one of the shells in the classroom, his big brown tail moving slowly behind him, as he was examining big maps, spread in front of him. He looked up as the sisters entered and smiled broadly.

"Oh, what a pleasant surprise! My favorite pupils have decided to visit me during their summer holidays!" He exclaimed.

"Yes, Teacher Arlo," Azalea said.

"There's something we'd like to ask you," Daisy interrupted, looking impatient.

"Really?" The teacher asked them, sounding interested. "It must be a very important thing if you've decided to come to school, to find and ask me. Well, I'm all ears. Go on. Ask."

Daisy and Azalea looked at each other, smiling. Azalea held the cloth in front of her, with the map side out, so that the teacher could only see the map.

"Teacher Arlo," she said. "This is a map that we've found somewhere…"

"Somewhere in one of our books," Daisy interrupted. Azalea threw her a disapproving glance.

"So," Azalea continued. "We would like to know where this place is. If you know about it, of course."

"But of course we're sure that you know because you're… a teacher. Of Worldology," Daisy said, sounding like a teacher herself.

"Hmm, let me see," the teacher said, swimming closer and putting on his glasses. "Let me see."

He narrowed his eyes and examined the map that Azalea was holding tightly.

"According to the lines drawn here, it seems to me that it's in the surroundings of the Three Thorn Reefs," he said after several minutes.

Azalea gasped. "Three Thorn Reefs?"

That place was famous for being dangerous, as many strange things were happening there. No one ever went to explore that place. There were three huge mountainous reefs situated like a triangle, but rather far from one another. There were myths that there were magical items at the feet of those mountains.

"So, now you know about the map, is there anything else you want to know?" The teacher asked.

Daisy looked at Azalea for a moment, and then said: "What do you know about the Three Thorn Reefs? I mean... there are many things that I've read in my books, but all of them are myths, aren't they?"

"Yes, I also personally think they're myths," the teacher said, going back and sitting down on his shell. "For example, the myth about the Pink Sparkle that grows you temporary legs," he added. "And that those sparkles are in special shells at the feet of those mountains."

"What?!" Daisy exclaimed, and then clapped a hand onto her mouth, her eyes wide.

The teacher was so deeply engrossed in the conversation, that he didn't even notice it.

"Then there are these poisonous medusas that live a bit higher in the upper waters," he said. "The myth is that if you eat water dahlia, you won't get poisoned."

"Oh, Teacher Arlo, that was so interesting!" Azalea exclaimed, looking at her teacher.

"By the way, why are you interested in the Three Thorn Reefs?" he asked, looking at them sternly.

"N… nothing, nothing at all," Azalea stammered.

"It was something we had come across and didn't know what it meant," Daisy said.

"Yes, like, we wanted to clarify," Azalea added, nodding fiercely.

"Well, in that case, I think I've clarified enough for you," the teacher said, smiling.

"Thank you so much, Teacher Arlo!" the sisters exclaimed, as they swam towards the exit of the classroom.

The teacher smiled and waved.

Daisy and Azalea were in the hallway, their eyes still wide open from the information they had got.

"Daisy, look, Teacher Arlo said that the medusas were poisonous..."

"But it's a myth, isn't it?" Daisy said, raising her eyebrows.

"Maybe, but in case it isn't, we must know that we can eat water dahlia," Azalea whispered. "It's we don't know where water dahlias grow."

Daisy frowned for a moment, and then she jumped up and down with joy.

"Azalea!" she whispered, barely able to keep her voice down, "The biology classroom! We can ask Teacher Calvin to lend us some. I know he has water dahlias in his cupboard …"

Azalea nodded, and they went into the next classroom.

Chapter 3

The Pink Sparkles

They had the water dahlia, and they had the map. The only thing left to do was to inform their parents that they would be absent for some time.

"Mom? dad?" Azalea called her parents, while Daisy was taking their small bags for the journey. "Daisy and I are going to take a long walk through Clover. We're not hungry, and we're not thirsty."

Their parents nodded and smiled, waving goodbye. "Don't stay too long," their mom said.

"And be careful," their dad said.

"All right," the sisters waved back and left the house. The map and the water dahlia were in Daisy's pink bag that was thrown over her shoulder. Azalea had her blue bag hang over her shoulder, too.

Hand in hand they swam out of Clover, got a bit far from their town and swam exactly towards the place that was called Three Thorn Reefs. The farther they swam from the town, the darker it got. There were no mermaids in the surroundings, and a few fish swam past by, indifferent to the sisters. Daisy got the map out and examined it.

"We're going in the right direction," she said, folding and putting it back into her bag.

"I can't believe we're doing this, Daisy," Azalea said.

"I'm glad we did everything for this," Daisy said. "Prince Zeke from Penetoland, we're coming!"

Giggling, the sisters swam until they reached the Three Thorn Reef. It was a huge black mountain, situated on the ocean floor and going all the way up to where Daisy and Azalea couldn't see.

"Wow," Daisy said, looking around.

"Daisy, don't you think it's a bit... dangerous?" Azalea said, her voice trembling a little. "Maybe we should go back home?"

"And leave poor Prince Zeke trapped on the island?" Daisy exclaimed. "No way."

"Well, of course, I don't want to leave him there…" Azalea said. "All right, let's do it!"

Daisy was searching for the surroundings of the mountains, looking in the corners and under the rocks.

"What are you looking for, Daisy?"

"The special shells that contain the magical sparkle," Daisy said.

"But it's a myth…"

"I don't know. I hope it isn't."

Something was sparkling under the rock, which caught Azalea's eyes. She swam closer and looked. It was a shell. Picking it up very carefully, Azalea opened it and couldn't believe her eyes – it was full of pink sparkle!

"D… Daisy!" She exclaimed. Daisy threw herself right at Azalea, impatient to see what was inside. She gasped audibly and clapped her hand onto her mouth.

"Azalea," she whispered, unable to look away from the magical pink sparkle. "So it was true!"

The two sisters looked at each other with wide-open eyes. Then, without a word, Daisy put her hand into the shell and took out a handful of pink sparkles.

"Daisy, are you sure you want to eat it?" A note of panic was heard in Azalea's voice, as Daisy took the sparkles to her mouth. She nodded and ate the sparkles. Both of them looked down at her tail.

"Nothing's happening!" Daisy said, getting frustrated. But then, as she was frowning in frustration, her tail started to transform. The sisters shrieked, as the tail became two beautiful legs. Daisy was wearing a pretty blue short skirt, exactly the color of her tail.

"Oh, my goodness! I have legs!" Daisy shook her legs in the water, excited and joyful. Azalea's eyes were sparkling. She also put a handful of sparkles into her mouth, and soon her pretty turquoise tail had become a short skirt for her two brand-new beautiful feet.

The sisters danced around, trying to walk in the water.

"Azalea, it's so easy to walk!" Daisy said, brandishing her legs to the sides. "And they are so beautiful!"

"Well, look, Daisy, now we have legs," Azalea said excitedly, "So now we can go and rescue the prince!"

"Yes, but the effect will wear off soon," Daisy said, looking around. "We'd better find some more magical shells and take them with us."

They looked under the small rocks and found a couple of shells. Azalea put them in her bag.

They tried to swim, but it was so difficult. They didn't have their tails, and shaking their feet didn't have the same effect as with the tails. They weren't used to having feet.

"I'm getting tired," Azalea said. "I don't think I can swim to the surface of the ocean with these feet."

"Me neither," Daisy said. "But the effect will wear off soon. Let's wait until we have our tails back, and then we'll swim up."

"Yes, and then we'll eat the sparkles again," Azalea added excitedly. The two sisters sat down on the bottom of the ocean, waiting. Some time passed.

"Daisy," Azalea said, "What if it was permanent?"

"What do you mean?" Daisy looked at her sister, frowning.

"What if we'll never grow back our tails and will have to live with these feet for the rest of our lives?" Azalea whispered.

Daisy's eyes got wider. "We didn't think about it…"

Then their feet transformed back into tails. The sisters breathed with relief. Azalea got up at once, shaking her tail, smiling.

"Wonderful!" She shrieked. "I was afraid we'd stay that way forever!"

"Now can we go, Azalea?" Daisy asked, shaking her tail happily.

"Let's go!" Azalea said, nodding and throwing her hands up.

Hand in hand, the sisters, swam upwards, smiling widely. It was the biggest adventure they were going to have in their lives, and they were very excited about it.

Chapter 4

The Splits

As they swam higher, it became lighter. Soon they were approaching the surface.

"Wait, Daisy!" Azalea said, suddenly stopping.

"What is it?"

"According to the myth, the poisonous medusas are about here," Azalea said. "Get the water dahlia from your bag, so we can eat it before approaching them."

Daisy quickly opened her bag and got out the water dahlia. Each of them took a few petals and ate them. The flower tasted semi-sweet and was very soft.

"I think this is enough," Azalea said. They continued swimming. Surely, there were many medusas near the surface of the ocean, at the reefs. The medusas were transparent, but the girls immediately saw them, as some of them came towards them.

"Ahh, Daisy!" Azalea shrieked, as one of the medusas bit her on the arm. "What shall I do now?"

Daisy swam to her sister, her eyes big with fear, and just then several medusas attacked her.

"Azalea, don't be afraid of them!" Daisy called, trying to push the medusas away from her. "Their poison can't do anything to us – we've eaten the flower!"

Azalea broke free from the group of hungry medusas and grabbed Daisy's hand. Together they quickly swam to the surface and got their heads out of the water. The medusas stayed behind. There was a big island in front of them, shining under the bright sunshine.

"So, this is Beyondness!" Daisy said, looking around in surprise. "I have never been out of the ocean before."

"Daisy, this is the magical island!" Azalea shouted with excitement.

"Let's swim to the island, quick!" Daisy said, shaking her tail vigorously.

Daisy and Azalea swam to the island and stopped near the seaside.

"Look, Azalea, let's eat the pink sparkle now, as it's getting impossible to swim – it's too shallow here."

Azalea took out one of the two remaining shells and opened it. Both of them took a handful of pink sparkles and ate it.

"I can't wait!" Daisy said, closing her eyes in excitement.

Their tails were replaced with feet and short skirts the color of their tails. The sisters stood, the water barely reaching their knees. Daisy tried to do a few steps, but it was more difficult to walk than it had seemed under the ocean.

Azalea was still standing, looking at her feet in surprise, when suddenly out of the waters a big shark appeared. The shark was swimming towards the sisters, with its mouth wide open, its sharp teeth visible.

"Azalea, run!" Daisy screamed and tried to run towards the island's sand, but it was very difficult, and she fell. Azalea didn't even try to run – she knew she couldn't run because she had never tried to. In her books about Beyondness, she had seen pictures of running people, but she didn't have any idea of how to do it.

"Hurry, Azalea!" Daisy was crawling towards the sands. For a second Azalea seemed petrified from fear, but then instinctively she threw the pink sparkle shell towards the shark.

"Get this, beast!" she screamed. She was aiming for the shark's head, hoping to make it dizzy, but the shell fell right into the shark's open mouth, the remaining pink sparkles sprinkling inside, and the shark swallowed involuntarily. The shark had almost reached Azalea, but it stopped moving for a moment.

Daisy and Azalea wondered what happened to it, and in front of their astonished eyes the shark's tail turned into two human feet, and it stood up, looking very surprised.

"What?!" Daisy exclaimed, looking at the shark, which had grown legs. The shark tried to move towards the girls, but it did the splits and fell into the water.

For a second the girls stood staring at the shark, which was struggling to stand up and was falling into the water all the time, and then they started laughing.

"Oh, look, Azalea!" Daisy was pointing to it and giggling, while Azalea almost fell into the water from laughter.

"A shark with legs!"

"Doing the splits!"

"Oh, look at his face!"

"Yeah, he's so surprised, like he has just won the Olympics!"

For a few moments, the girls were having fun with the confused shark, when suddenly Azalea remembered that the feet effect was temporary.

"Let's go, quick!" She said, trying to walk out of the water. "We don't have much time! The shark will soon acquire his tail again."

"Besides, we'll acquire our tails, too, while we're there on the island, and will be stuck on the island forever!" Daisy said, and Azalea couldn't tell if Daisy was excited or worried about it.

"Daisy, calm down, we still have one more shell of pink sparkles," Azalea said quietly.

At last, they were out of the water.

"You're doing a funny dance, Azalea," Daisy said, giggling, seeing that her sister was trying to walk. She had already mastered the basics of walking and now was feeling very self-confident.

"Wait till I learn how to run!" Azalea said, trying to improve.

The girls crossed the area of sand and reached a place full of trees.

"Is this a forest?" Daisy asked, looking at the thick trees in front of them. "I think I've read about forests in my book of Beyondness."

"I've also read about them," Azalea said, coming forward, but at that moment the trees came closer together, closing the way with their branches, making it impossible to walk.

"What's happening?" Daisy asked, coming closer and looking at the trees. There were fruits on the branches.

"I don't know..." Azalea answered. The more they tried to pass through the branches, the more the branches intertwined, leaving no space to walk through. They even tried to walk a bit along the seashore, to find another way in, but the entire island seemed to be circled with the same type of trees. Suddenly the nearest tree's truck turned into a gap, which looked like a mouth. The mouth started talking:

"Oh, see who has come! Pretty girls! And I think you want to pass through my branches, don't you? But before I let you pass, you must do something for me."

Chapter 5

Obstacles Are for Overcoming

"Azalea! The tree can talk!" Daisy exclaimed.

Azalea was looking with her mouth open. "Daisy, I haven't read about talking trees in my Beyondness book!"

Daisy rummaged in her small bag and took out the prince's letter.

"Azalea, he's written that this is a strange island," she said. "Maybe he meant this?"

Azalea came a bit forward and looked at the tree trunk.

"Hello, tree, yes we want to pass through the branches," she said. "What shall we do for you to let us pass?"

The tree was silent for a couple of minutes.

"Daisy, I can't believe I'm talking with a tree," Azalea said, barely holding her laughter.

Daisy giggled. The tree trunk started talking again:

"You must think about what you can do for me. You must earn the way into the island. Otherwise, you will stay on that side of the island."

The sisters looked at each other and shrugged.

"Look, tree," Daisy said. "You want us to do something? Well, we can pick the fruit from your branches and eat them. You will be lighter, and we'll not be hungry anymore..."

"Hey," the tree said, "By eating my fruit, you're not doing any good to me – only to you. Think again."

"Um, I think we can cut off your unnecessary branches," Azalea said, her eyes brightening at her genius idea.

"Cut off my branches?"

"Unnecessary ones…"

"I don't have any unnecessary branches," the tree said. "Just like your fingers and toes, all my branches are useful and not at all unnecessary."

Daisy and Azalea sat down on the sand and started to think. Then their feet vanished and tails grew in their place.

"Oh, no!" Daisy exclaimed. "Come on, Azalea, let's eat the remaining sparkles."

The sisters opened the last shell and ate the pink sparkles. Suddenly Daisy's face brightened.

"Azalea!" she shrieked, looking at the empty shell. "We can water the tree with this shell!"

Before Azalea could say anything, the tree said:

"Good for you! You're correct."

The sisters got up and went to the ocean to bring some water with the shell. The tree was contented and opened the way for them. As the forest ended, they appeared in front of a big mountain, the top of which could hardly be seen.

"Daisy, I think this island gives us obstacles to pass."

"And we pass them," Daisy said with determination. The sisters started to climb up the mountain. It was very difficult for them, because they had only learned how to walk, and climbing up a mountain was too difficult. They had to adjust their knees and toes and to hold onto the rocks to keep themselves from falling. The mountain wasn't too steep, so the sisters managed to climb half of it without any accidents. They had almost reached the top – there was just a little bit to climb when Daisy felt her feet starting to transform into a tail.

"Azalea!" she shrieked, unable to stand on the rock. Azalea turned just in time to see her sister slipping. Her tail was starting to appear instead of her feet, but she was holding onto a big rock securely, her right arm wrapped around it. Instinctively she threw her left hand towards her sister and grabbed her hair just as Daisy was falling.

"Ouch! My hair!" Daisy screamed.

"I've got you, Daisy! I'm holding you!" Azalea shrieked happily. Daisy was dangling from her hair in Azalea's hands, her tail shaking violently, and finally, she managed to grab hold of one of the small rocks that were sticking out from the mountain's sides. Azalea lets go of her hair, seeing that her sister was safely back onto the mountain again.

"Oh, my goodness! It was so horrible!" Daisy said. "We need more sparkles."

"Unfortunately we don't have any, Daisy... But we are strong, and we still have our arms!"

Daisy looked at her sister and nodded with determination. "Whatever happens, we shall never give up!"

"We can do anything if we put our mind to it!" Azalea added.

The two sisters continued climbing, even only using their arms and tails, and eventually, they reached the top. The top of the mountain was rather spacey. There was a fast river flowing around the top, and there was another, smaller island in the center of the crazy river. There were several trees on the island, but it was a bit far from the bank the girls were standing, so they couldn't see what exactly there was.

"Do you think the prince is on the island?" Daisy asked.

"I hope so. Where else can he be? I guess he didn't even have to pass through all those obstacles, as he has arrived here by an air balloon."

"Yeah, most probably he has landed right in the middle of this smaller island," Daisy said.

"Well, I'm really glad that there's a river here," Azalea said, sitting down on the river bank. "We can swim."

The river was flowing violently, deafening the surroundings with its loud rumble; crazy waves are splashing here and there. The river seemed to go round and round, around the small island in the center of it. There were broken branches, oddly-shaped rocks and lots of leaves, flowing with the river, giving it a scary look.

"Azalea, I think it's going to be dangerous to swim in this river…" Daisy said slowly.

"Yeah, looks like it," Azalea nodded.

"But I'm sure we can do it," Daisy said after some time. "If we were able to climb up a mountain without feet, then we can swim in this violent river, too."

"I agree with you," Azalea said, nodding. "Ultimately, we'll have to rescue the prince."

"Yes, now I can see why poor prince hasn't been able to get out of the island," Daisy said, pointing the river with her finger. "Because of this."

"Let's go, Daisy. Try to be careful," Azalea said, getting near the edge of the river bank. Daisy pushed herself closer to her sister.

"On the count of three – one… two… three!"

The sisters pushed themselves off the bank and into the crazy river. At first, the flow took control over them, splashing violently, but the sisters quickly gained control of themselves and managed to swim, shaking their pretty tails in the water, making the waves obey them. They were dodging and avoiding the heavy objects in the water, sometimes diving deep into the water, and sometimes coming out on the surface when it wasn't dangerous. The sisters were getting tired, but the island was closer now, which gave them hope. They were panting and were so exhausted that couldn't speak with each other while swimming.

Chapter 6

The Golden Crown

At last, they reached the island and pulled themselves out of the water. They sat on the bank of the river and looked around in surprise: it was a beautiful island, with singing birds and colorful butterflies flying in the air, with many trees and flowers growing in the dense grass on the ground. The trees were full of sweet-looking fruits, and the air was clean and fresh up there. The sisters took some rest there.

"Now what?" Daisy asked. "This is a wonderful place, but where's the prince?"

Azalea also looked a bit frustrated. "Well, I hope we haven't come here in vain… after all the obstacles that we overcame."

"You, know, even if it was in vain, Azalea, now we're stronger and know that we can do anything!" Daisy said proudly. "Don't you think so?"

"I think you're right, Daisy. We have learned that determination and the dream to reach your goal are the most important things to reach the goal in reality."

"So even if we don't find the prince here, we'll go back the way we came, and will always remember this as the craziest adventure we have ever had," Daisy said, but there was a note of sadness in her voice. "I wish that Prince Zeke was here…"

Their conversation was interrupted by a loud whistle.

"Prince Zeke, there are two mermaids speaking about you," a loud voice croaked, making the sisters jump up startled.

"That's impossible, Mr. Palm-Tree," a young boy's voice was heard nearby. "How can mermaids be here? This is the top of a mountain, and the mermaids can't climb up the mountains, nor can they fly."

Daisy raised her eyebrows and looked at astonished Azalea. They turned around and saw the talking palm tree that was near them. The prince couldn't be seen.

"I'm telling you, Prince Zeke," the tree said, "They've come to rescue you. If you don't believe me, come and see yourself."

The bushes parted, and a young boy appeared with a golden crown on his head. He was blond, with freckles and blue eyes. He was almost their age. The prince looked at them, staring at their mermaid tails. He closed his eyes, then opened them again and looked at the mermaid sisters, a look of utmost surprise on his face.

"Is… is this a dream?" he asked. "Or a mirage?"

Daisy and Azalea were looking back at him, equally dumbstruck. They were seeing a human being for the first time in their lives.

"Are you real mermaids?" The prince asked. "I know this is a magical island, but I had no idea that it also had mermaids living on it."

"We don't live on this island," Azalea said, coming back to her senses, while Daisy was still staring. "My name is Azalea, and this is my sister Daisy. We've come to rescue you."

"To rescue me?" the prince whispered. "So you've found my note?"

Azalea nodded.

"I can't believe that of all people, two beautiful mermaid sisters would come to rescue me," the prince exclaimed, giggling happily. "But how did you get here? This small island is on top of a high mountain."

"That's our little secret," Daisy said, who had also woken up from her initial state of shock.

"Now the question is – how are we going to rescue you?" Azalea said. "Can you swim, Prince Zeke?"

"No," he said. "That's the reason I got stuck here. Look at that horrible river!"

"We thought so," Daisy said. "Of course we'll help you swim through it," she added with a serious look on her face.

The prince looked at her incredulously. "Are you serious? I can't swim…"

"Don't worry," Azalea said. "If you're with us, then everything will be all right."

"Let's go then," Daisy said, "Azalea and I will hold onto your arms, and you will swim with us."

The prince knew he had no other choice. These two mermaids were his only rescuers.

"Goodbye, Mr. Palm-Tree," he said, waving. "Thank you for feeding me."

"Goodbye, Prince Zeke, be careful. Visit me from time to time," the tree said.

The Prince held the mermaid sisters' hands and took a deep breath. The sisters held his hands tightly and jumped into the river.

"Oh, wow!" the prince started screaming the moment they hit the water. Daisy and Azalea were doing their best to keep his head over the surface. The river was as violent as before. The crazy waves were crushing on their heads, making them go down for a few seconds, before coming up again. Suddenly the prince's golden crown fell off his head. The waves seemed to be throwing it to one another, playing with it.

"Oh, no! My crown! My golden crown!" The prince shouted and, forgetting that he couldn't swim, threw himself after his crown. Daisy and Azalea followed him, but the waves had taken the prince and were rushing him to the other side of the island. The sisters had never been to the other side of the small island. What they saw there, was more than they could have imagined.

Chapter 7

The Best Day

A huge, breathtaking waterfall was starting from there and falling right into the ocean. The entire ocean could be seen from such height. The sisters screamed as they saw the prince at last grab his crown, but he was already on the edge of the waterfall. Daisy threw herself towards him and grabbed his outstretched hand while Azalea caught Daisy's other hand.

Together they started to fall down the waterfall, which was so high the bottom couldn't be seen because of the white froth and dense fog.

Shrieking and screaming, the sisters and the prince were almost flying all the way down the waterfall. Their voices could hardly be heard, as the waterfall was very noisy. There were a few birds flying over the waterfall and were looking in surprise at the two mermaids and the prince, flying in the air and screaming.

"Daisy!" Azalea screamed through the mist, "I can't believe we're falling down a waterfall!"

"This is like a dream, Azalea!" Daisy called.

The prince was still screaming on top of his lungs, with his eyes tightly shut and his mouth wide open.

At last, the waterfall came to its end. The mermaids and the prince fell into the ocean with a loud splash. They got down a little, and then the water threw the prince up. The sisters followed him to the surface of the ocean. The prince was breathless and looking around frantically. He was still holding tightly his golden crown, because of which they had discovered a new way out of the strange island.

"Wow! That was magical!" He said, at last, smiling happily. "You saved me from that island, Daisy, and Azalea."

"Yes, we did, but now we have to save you again – we're in the middle of the ocean," Azalea said.

"How can we get you to your kingdom, Prince Zeke?" Daisy asked him.

"Well, I don't know… it's supposed to be not too far from here, anyway," the prince said slowly. "But I think I'm learning how to swim because of you!"

The mermaid sisters giggled.

"I wish we could take you to Clover, our town, down in the ocean," Daisy said. "Too bad, you can't breathe underwater."

The prince didn't have time to answer because at that moment they noticed a pretty dolphin swimming their way.

"Hey, I think I'm seeing two mermaids and a boy in the middle of the ocean!" the dolphin exclaimed.

"Hi," the mermaid sisters waved happily.

The prince was looking at the mermaids and the dolphin, not understanding their language. "Are you speaking with that dolphin?" he asked Daisy.

"Oh, yes, we can understand fish language," Daisy said. "We're mermaids, remember?"

The dolphin smiled kindly.

"And who is this boy? A new mermaid?" the dolphin asked.

"No, he's the Prince of Penetoland," Azalea said. "He was lost, we found him, but now we don't know how to take him back to his kingdom."

"The Prince?" The dolphin repeated. "There are many ships out there, looking for the prince. All of the ships are the Kingdom's ships. So here he is!"

Daisy and Azalea looked at each other in astonishment. So there were ships looking for the prince. It would be so easy to take him there!

As if reading their mind, the dolphin said: "I can show you the way, if you want."

"Yes, of course!" Daisy exclaimed while Azalea nodded happily.

"Come with us, Prince Zeke," the girls told him. "This dolphin will show us the way to your Kingdom's ships. They are looking for you all over the ocean."

"Are they?" The Prince asked happily, his eyes sparkling with joy.

The mermaid sisters, the prince, and the dolphin, set off to swim towards the ships. The dolphin helped the prince swim. Soon they noticed many ships scattered in the ocean. They swam to the biggest of them and stopped by the ship.

"Thank you so much, dear dolphin!" Azalea said, smiling.

"Here they are," the dolphin said, waved and swam away.

"The prince! He's there! He's alive! He's safe! Let's get him on board!" People started yelling at the ship when they noticed them in the water.

"Daisy, Azalea," the prince said, turning to the sisters. "I'm so thankful to you for saving me. I could never have imagined that I could ever meet mermaids, as I didn't even know that they existed. But now I've met two of the kindest, cleverest and bravest mermaids in the world," he added.

The sisters smiled and nodded.

"We're glad that we're the ones to rescue you because it was the biggest and the most interesting adventure that we've ever had in our lives," Daisy said.

"Today we did things we could never imagine we'd ever do," Azalea added. "We'll always remember this day. Thank you, too, for giving us the opportunity to save you."

The prince also smiled. The sisters waited until the prince was pulled on board. Then they waved at him and dived into the water. They swam deep down until they reached Clover. Hurriedly, they entered their house, where there were their parents.

"Daisy, Azalea, you're just in time for dinner," their mom said. "You look so happy. Has something good happened?"

The sisters looked at each other, smiling.

"Mom, today I and Azalea understood what it meant to be kind."

"And what determination meant," Azalea added.

"Also, we learned that if you have a goal, then you can reach it, no matter what," Daisy said.

"The only thing you need is patience."

"And will-power…"

"And that you must be brave, strong, courageous…"

Their mom was looking at her daughters with admiration.

"My girls, I'm so glad for you. Everything that I would want you to know, you've learned today and are happy for it."

*****

That night when the sisters went to bed, each of them took their copies of the book about Beyondness.

"Now I understand how they walk," Daisy said in a tired and sleepy but happy voice.

"I will always remember that waterfall – it was so breathtaking," Azalea said, smiling softly.

"This was the best adventure ever. Even the shark that was doing the splits," Daisy said, "I hope he has grown his tail already."

The girls giggled and turned off the light. The smile on their faces, they fell asleep, full of exciting and crazy memories of one very interesting day in their life.

THE END

Conclusion

Diana Molly is a writer for children who enjoy writing as much as reading. Her books mainly focus on friendship, efforts and good lessons. She believes that children learn from books, and any good book is like a good friend that can give only good advice. The number one reader of her stories is her own daughter, who enjoys her mother's stories and always waits for more to come.

Diana Molly likes the story of Paper Bag Princess and believes that girls can be adventurous and strong, instead of being weak and fearful. The young readers can see this reflected in her stories, where the girls are the main heroes and solve problems better than many boys could have done.

Made in the USA
Coppell, TX
29 April 2020

23420114R00037